SPACE TORTOISE

Written by
Ross Montgomery

Illustrated by
David Litchfield

First published in the UK in 2018
by Faber and Faber Limited
Bloomsbury House, 74–77 Great Russell Street,
London WC1B 3DA

Text © Ross Montgomery, 2018

Illustrations © David Litchfield, 2018

PB ISBN 978–0–571–33105–5

Printed in Europe

The moral rights of Ross Montgomery
and David Litchfield have been asserted.

A CIP record for this book is available from
the British Library

10 9 8 7 6 5 4 3 2 1

FSC
www.fsc.org

MIX
Paper from
responsible sources
FSC® C022612

Once, in an old rusty bin
in an old rusty playground
in an old empty park,
there lived a little tortoise.

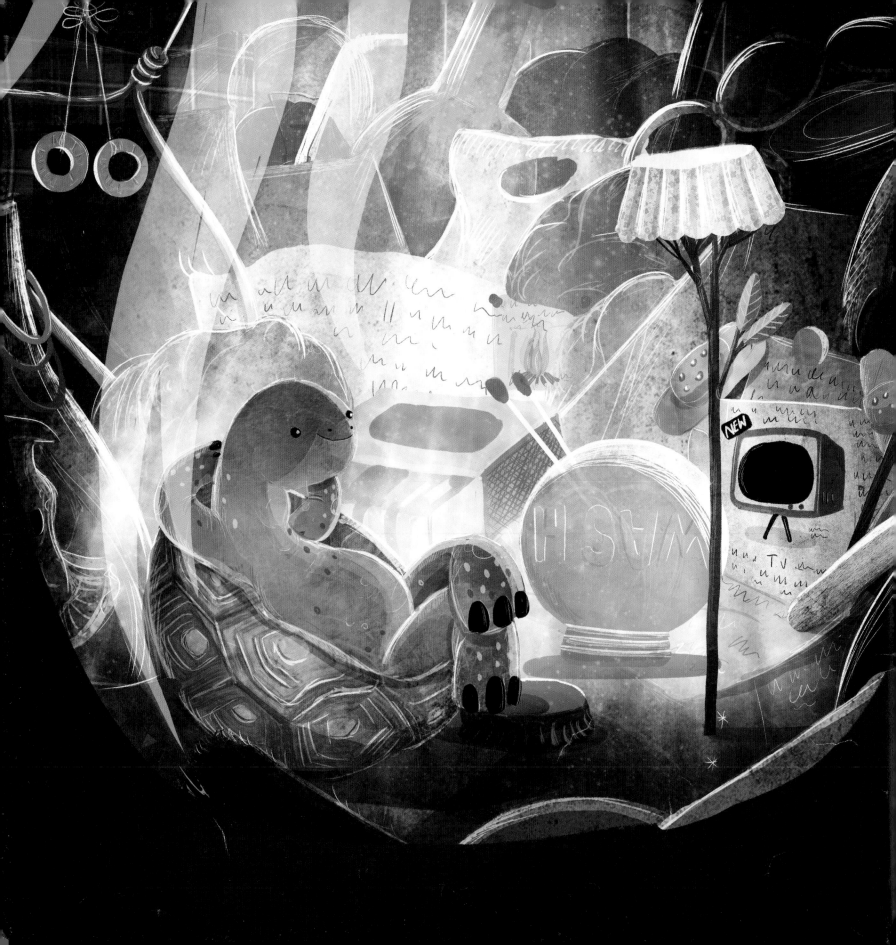

The tortoise's bin was cosy, warm
and dry all year round, even in winter.

What more could a little tortoise need?

But the tortoise never saw any other animals in the park. Sometimes he would search for them in the long grass . . .

And on top of the slide . . .

And under the swings . . .

But he never found them.

One night, the tortoise was gazing
up at the sky.

"Look at those candles glowing up there," he said to himself. "That must be where the other animals are . . . I wish I could join them."

But how could a little tortoise get to the top of the sky?

The next day, the tortoise found an old book in his bin.
It was filled with pictures of space rockets.

"So that's what I need to get to the top of the sky," he said. "But where will I find a rocket?"

The tortoise peeked out of his bin. And there,
right in front of the moon was . . .

A rocket!

The little tortoise picked up his candle
and set off across the park.

Soon the tortoise came to a desert. It stretched far into the horizon, silent as a whisper.

He made his way across the dunes, past broken statues and crumbling castles.

The tortoise came to a great
wide ocean. The wind had whipped
the waves into a furious storm.

The tortoise was afraid, but there was no turning back now. He found a boat and set its sails to the wind.

At last, the tortoise came to the farthest shore. There was the rocket, right in front of him!

It towered above the little tortoise, too high to climb.

But he had an idea.

The tortoise searched
through a bin until he found
what he needed.

Then he sewed
and cut and
tightened
and twisted.

The balloon glowed like a tiny star as it
carried the little tortoise up through the night sky.

The tortoise floated through the clouds,
right up to the rocket's tip.

But there was a problem.
He couldn't see the
cockpit anywhere . . .
Or the boosters . . .
OR the fuel tank . . .

"What a strange rocket,"
said the tortoise.

"I'm sorry to disturb you,"
said a voice. "But this isn't a rocket."

The tortoise turned around.
On the ledge was a tiny mouse.

"What are you doing up here?" said
the tortoise, taken by surprise.

"I'm looking at the stars."
The mouse smiled. "Beautiful, aren't they?"

The tortoise frowned. "Stars?
You mean . . . those lights up there aren't
candles being held by other animals?"

"No," said the mouse. "There are no
animals in the sky – just stars."

The tortoise hung his head. "Oh dear."

And he turned away to go home.

"Wait!" said the mouse. "Why don't you stay for tea? My house is right there! See?"

The tortoise couldn't believe
his eyes. Behind the clock tower,
on the other side of the park, there
were hundreds of little animal
houses, each one lit by a candle.

In fact, the candles looked
just like stars.